T. Herbert Warren

By Severn Sea

And other Poems

T. Herbert Warren

By Severn Sea
And other Poems

ISBN/EAN: 9783744722476

Printed in Europe, USA, Canada, Australia, Japan

Cover: Foto ©Andreas Hilbeck / pixelio.de

More available books at **www.hansebooks.com**

BY SEVERN SEA

AND OTHER POEMS

T. HERBERT WARREN, M.A.

President of Magdalen College, Oxford

JOHN MURRAY, ALBEMARLE STREET

1898

TO THE QUEEN

LADY WHOSE ORBED SOVEREIGNTY
    BY MANY A LAND AND EVERY SEA
    TIES HALF THE GLOBE WITH EMPERY,

WHO ASKED OF HEAVEN THE BETTER PART,
    A WISE AND UNDERSTANDING HEART,
    AND GAINED LONG LIFE AND RULING ART ;

NOW WHEN HER FLOWERS A NATION FLINGS,
    NOW WHEN THE WORLD ITS GREETING BRINGS,
    AND WITH ACCLAIM A PLANET RINGS :

ONE BLOOM HER CLOISTER-GARDEN BEARS,
    ONE ECHO OF HER CHANTED AIRS,
    YOUR COLLEGE OF THE LILY DARES

ON THIS TWICE CROWNED CROWNING DAY
    THAT SUMS THE CYCLES OF YOUR SWAY
    LOYALLY AT YOUR FEET TO LAY.

Magdalen College, Oxford :
20th June, 1897.

TABLE OF CONTENTS

Table of Contents

Table of Contents

NOTE.—*Some of the pieces which follow are reprinted by permission from the " Spectator," " Athenæum," and " Guardian," and from " Macmillan's " and the " Oxford Magazine," in which they first appeared. The greater number of them formed the collection issued in a small limited edition in the spring of this year (1897) by Mr. Daniel of Worcester College, Oxford, from his private press, but a few are now printed for the first time.*

TO R. D. BLACKMORE

PROSE POET of the fabled West,
    Ere school and railway had begun
    To fuse our shires and tongues in one,
And equalize the worst and best,

While Devon vowels fluted yet
        By Dart and Lynn their mellow length,
        While flourished still in Saxon strength
The consonants of Somerset,

Your Exmoor epic fixed the hues
        That lingered on by combe and tor,
        And in the hollow vale of Oare
You found a matter for your Muse !

The brigands' den, the prisoned bride,
        The giant yeoman's hero mould,
        Who fought and garrulously told
The Iliad of his country-side ;

B   I

You bade them live and last for us
        And for our heirs, as caught erewhile
        The Doric of his rocky isle
Lives in your loved Theocritus ;—

Loved, for you are a child of ours,
        And know and prize the scholar's home
        Who learned in student days to roam
Among the cloisters and the towers

Where now my missive rhyme I pen
        To greet you as in lettered ease
        You move amid your birds and bees,
Old Virgil's gardener come again ;

Or like Alcinous from his hall
        Survey your orchards ripening fair,
        Apple on apple, pear on pear,
From snowy blossom to golden ball ;

Or teach your swelling vines to shape
        Their tender buds and safely thrust
        The spires that hold in starry dust
The promise of the purple grape.

'   So may they find you, may you take
            These verses with a kindlier eye
            And backward thoughts of sympathy
    With him who writes, for memory's sake ;

    Who loves like you the western ground,
            The wilder scene, the hills that scent
            The sea, and in this inland pent
    That hems our Academe around,

    Must fain require his haunts of old,
            Though happy here, and sometimes miss
            By still and silver Tamesis
    The rushing Severn's molten gold.

                    Oxford:
                        April, 1896.

3

BY SEVERN SEA

THE rolling moorland russet-dun
      With all its gold and purple bloom
Made fragrant by the summer sun,
      Climbs from the softly-curving combe
      Above dark wood and whitening lea
      And orchard green by Severn Sea ;

A noble flood, more proudly wide,
      From our dear island's mother breast
Pours none, nor swirls a fuller tide
      To barter with the boundless West
      For many a costly argosy
      Than this broad stream of Severn Sea.

A dateless gulf whose wave of old
      Yet fervent from the central flame,
By tropic jungle steaming rolled,
      Or foamed around the monstrous frame
      Of flying, creeping, swimming things
      With serpent gorge and dragon wings ;

4

Lands that a mystic glamour fills,
    The after-glow of sunken stars,
Where the old tongues murmur to the hills
    Dead loves, dead hates, forgotten wars,
      And Arthur's phantom glories haunt
      The shadowy scene of high romaunt.

What life, what death of brute and man
    Have scarred your earth and stained your wave,
Where pirate horde and robber clan
    Have reared and ravaged home and grave,
      And gorgeous wrecks of stately Spain
      Mix with the bones of Celt and Dane !

Now all is peace from shore to shore,
    Mourns Avalon in ruined state
Beneath her silent-watching tor,
    And holy Cleeve thy sculptured gate
      Sees but the glittering runnel pass
      Beside thy cloister-guarded grass ;

While towered hall and castle stand,
    Their ancient wont and fashion yet

Unchanged, as if some fairy hand
    'Mid their green oaks of Somerset
    Had lulled them to such drowsihood
    As chained erewhile the Slumbering Wood,

So sleep they, only through their dream
    At times the merry bugles wind,
When hound and horse and horseman gleam
    By ferny haunts of hart and hind,
    And pride of olden venerie
    The antlered stag goes wildly free.

Nought hear they else, but from its well
    Deep in the dim heart of the glen
The secret stream from dell to dell
    Rustling by ways apart from men,
    Till in some cool and shadowed cave
    It wed the quiet-waiting wave.

O charmèd realm, O storied scene,
    What echoes whisper on your tide,
What memories mingle with your sheen,
    Of lives that here have breathed and died,

Of lips whose unforgotten lays
Made beauty lovelier by their praise !

Here sojourned erst the lyric three,
    Whose wandering made a classic ground
From Quantoxhead to Dunkery,
    Where they by height or hollow found
    Fountains that carol for all time
    In tune to their own deathless rhyme ;

And here that nearer dearer tongue
    Mourned his dead friend and sang the dirge—
More sadly sweet was never sung—
    Of him who on your murmurous verge
    Wind-wafted from Italian land
    Hath rest by his own Severn strand.

Ah western winds and waters mild !
    Others your vaporous languors chide ;
They have not loved you from a child,
    Nor grown to strength your shore beside.
    Ye speak of youth and hope to me,
    Ye airs, ye floods of Severn Sea !

7

For I was native to your mood
    And apt to take your influence,
To muse and pause, to pore and brood,
      To doubt the shows and shapes of sense,
      To dream how not to dream away
      The long large hours of boyhood's day.

And when high noon on many a sail
    Was bright along the brimming flow,
Or when the westering sun must fail
      Blood-red, and from the shifting glow
      Of lilac-citron skies the queen
      That sways your motion glimmered green,

One lesson still my spirit learned
    From flood and daylight fleeting past,
And from its own strange self that yearned
      Like them to lapse into the vast,
      And merge and end its vague unrest
      In some wide ocean of the West ;

Ere we can find true peace again,
    Our being must have second birth,

8

Purged and made one through joy and pain
    With Him Who rules and rounds the earth,
    Beyond the dark, behind the light,
    In mystery of the Infinite.

And we like rivers from their source
    Through cloud and shine, by deep or shoal,
Must follow that which draws our course,
    The Love that is its guide and goal ;
    Of life, of death, ye made me free,
    Waters and hills of Severn Sea !

                Minehead:
                August, 1892.

TO LORD TENNYSON

NESTOR of Poesy, whose utterance sage
    Has charmed so long our time, example bright
  In the hard war of Truth, a steadfast light
To guide our search in this self-darkened age !
Thou in a more heroic hour didst wage
    With men of mighty mould victorious fight
    Two generations back, and still of right
Reign'st in the third, and none may lift thy gage ;

Nor yet in this thy lovely Pylian realm
    And hospitable home, wilt wholly rest,
      Shaping what shall not die, beside the shore,
Till God shall bid thee sail and bend the helm
    Beyond the Ocean and the misty West,
      Whither thine own Antilochus went before.

Freshwater :

April, 1891.

VIRGILIUM VIDI

THE old Latin commentators preserve several striking notices of Virgil's habit of reading or reciting his poems, both while he was composing them, and after they were completed, and especially of the remarkable beauty and charm of the poet's rendering of his own words and its powerful effect upon his hearers. ' He read,' says Suetonius, ' at once with sweetness and with a wonderful fascination; and Seneca had a story of the poet Julius Montanus saying that he himself would attempt to steal something from Virgil if he could first borrow his voice, his elocution, and his dramatic power in reading; for the very same lines, said he, which when the author himself read them sounded well, without him were empty and dumb. He read to Augustus the whole of his Georgics, *and on another occasion three books of the Æneid, the second, the fourth, and the sixth, the last with an effect upon Octavia not to be forgotten, for she was present at the reading, and at those great lines about her own son and his premature death, which begin "* Tu Marcellus eris," *it is said that she fainted away and was with difficulty recovered. His amanuensis Eros again, in his old age, used to relate how Virgil, on one occasion, carried away by the warmth of recitation, had completed on*

11

the spur of the moment two lines previously left by him unfinished,
—the lines—

    Misenum Æoliden, quo non præstantior alter

    Ære ciere viros, Martemque accendere cantu—

and had ordered him at once to write them into the book.' (SUET.
Life of Virgil, ed. Nettleship, *pp.* 15, 16.) *Another passage*
which Virgil is said to have read, with immense effect upon the
*feelings of his hearers, is the well-known one in the fourth Æ*neid
(*vv.* 320-324).

    Te propter Lybicæ gentes Nomadumque tyranni

    Odere, infensi Tyrii ; te propter eundem

    Exstinctus pudor, et, qua sola sidera adibam,

    Fama prior.   Cui me moribundam deseris, hospes ?

    Hoc solum nomen quoniam de conjuge restat.

                             (SERVIUS *ad loc.*)

TO ALFRED LORD TENNYSON

LORD in this land and lord in many lands,
　　However far may reach
The myriad labour or our English hands,
　　Our always-widening speech,
Crowned with the bay and brightening with your fame
　　The leaves your elders wore !
Now while the crocus darts a leaping flame,
　　About your garden-door,
And by your trees the flower, whose happy part
　　Time since it was to fill
With her blithe mood a sterner laureate's heart,
　　The gracious daffodil, ,
Coy daughter of the wild and wont to hide
　　A shy and secret queen,
Springs unafraid and flaunts her simple pride
　　Of sylvan gold and green ;
While on the downs above the wintry turf
　　The venturous violets peep,
And with a softer sigh the creaming surf
　　Seethes round the chalky steep,

13

And on his cheek the climbing traveller feels
    Not quite unkind the breeze
Before whose breath a bluer shadow steals
    Across the thawing seas,
And in the sheltered combes beside the snow
    The first primroses dare,
And the lark flutes and flutters high and low
    Tossed on the April air ;
Now when the singing and the springing time
    Makes bolder every heart,
Take, king of verse, the tribute of a rhyme,
    Albeit of little art,
From one who prizes more than words can say,
    As life and cares grow long,
What charmed with simpler spell his boyhood's day—
    The magic of your song ;
As more and more a wiser sense divines
    What in quick heats of youth
He deemed the form of beauty in your lines
    To be the soul of truth :
And counts him thrice and four times fortunate
    To have found such signal grace
Of welcome bidding pass the sacred gate,
    And entering, face to face

14

To have seen the Virgil of our time, and heard,
    More musical than song,
The rolling cadence of the poet's word
    In accents true and strong,
Grandly reverberant with a nation's wail
    Above the warrior's grave,
Or softly calling to the silver sail
    Across the moonlit wave ;
In such a moving voice as that which made
    The imperial mother swoon
With sweet and sharp of sorrow, when it bade
    The purple flowers be strewn,
And lavish lilies heaped upon the head
    Withdrawn as soon as shown,
Rome's idle honour to a spirit fled
    Too pure to be her own ;
Or sang how piled beneath Misenus' hill
    The trumpet and the oar
Signed the dumb ghost whose living lips had skill
    To light the blaze of war ;
The very voice of beauty and of art
    Where yet so strangely ring
Those undernotes of tears that are a part
    Of every mortal thing.

15

Dust is the singer, but the song endures,
    Making the old tongue of Rome,
Though dead, to speak ; and even so shall yours
    O'erleap the bounds of home,
Not only to be read by him who spells
    A half-forgotten lore
'Mid mouldering shelves of ancient halls, or dwells
    Upon an old-world shore,
Beside some classic hill or fount that links
    Our day to ages flown
By Tuscan or Ægean wave, or drinks
    The Danube or the Rhone,
But echoing round and round our ampler earth
    To capes of hope and ire,
And islands parted by the globe's full girth,
    And zones of frost and fire,
Where Mississippi or Saint Lawrence drifts
    His rafted forests by,
Or snowy-corniced Himalaya lifts
    The world's white roof on high.

Freshwater :
    April, 1891.

IN MEMORIAM

ALFRED LORD TENNYSON

Μοῦσα καινῶν ὕμνων
ἄεισον ἐν δακρύοις
ᾠδὰν ἐπικήδειον.

L AST left of the mortal Immortals, art thou too taken at
    last,
Loved part so long of the present, must thou too pass to the
    past ?
Thou hast lain in the moonlight and lapsed in a glory from
    rest into rest,
And still is the teeming brain, and the warm heart cold in the
    breast,
And frozen the exquisite fancy, and mute the magical tongue
From our century's tuneful morn to its hushing eve that had
    sung.

Crowned poet and crown of poets whose wealth and whose wit
    could combine
Great echoes of old-world Homer, the grandeur of Milton's
    line,

The sad sweet glamour of Virgil, the touch of Horace divine,
Theocritus' musical sigh, and Catullus daintily fine !

Poet of Art and of Nature, of sympathies old and new,
Who read in the earth and the heavens, the fair and the good
    and the true,
And who wrote no line and no word that the world will ever
    rue !
Singer of God and of men, the stars were touched by thy
    brow,
But thy feet were on English meadows, true singer of England
    thou !
We lose thee from sight, but thy brothers with honour receive
    thee now,
From earliest Chaucer and Spenser to those who were nearer
    allied,
The rainbow-radiance of Shelley and Byron's furious pride,
Rich Keats and austere Wordsworth, and Browning who
    yesterday died
By sunny channels of Venice, and Arnold from Thames' green
    side.

Knells be rung, and wreaths be strung, and dirges be sung for
    the laurelled hearse,

Our tears and our flowers fade scarce more fast than our
transient verse,
For even as the refluent crowds from the glorious Abbey
disperse,
They are all forgotten, and we go back to our fleeting lives ;
But we are the dying, and thou the living, whose work
survives,
The sum and the brief of our time, to report to the after-years
Its thoughts and its loves and its hopes and its doubts and its
faiths and its fears ;
They live in thy lines for ever, and well may our era rejoice
To speak to the ages to come with so sweet and so noble a
voice.

12th October, 1892.

ADDISON'S WALK

GREEN natural cloister of our Academe,
   What ghost is this that greets us as we pace
   Beneath your boughs, the genius of the place,
With soft accost that fits our musing dream ?
Scholar, divine, or statesman would beseem
      That reverend air, that pensive-brilliant face
      And lofty wit and speech of Attic grace
Rich in grave ornament and noble theme :

'Tis he who played unspoiled a worldly part,
   Taught the town truth, and in a formal age
      Lured fop and toast to heed a note sublime ;
Who here had early learned the crowning art,
   To walk the world like Plato's monarch-sage,
      Spectator of all being and all time.

20

MAY-DAY ON MAGDALEN TOWER

WRITTEN FOR
MR. HOLMAN HUNT'S PICTURE

M ORN of the year, of day and May the prime !
How fitly do we scale the steep dark stair,
Into the brightness of the matin air,
To praise with chanted hymn and echoing chime,
Dear Lord of Light, Thy lowlihead sublime
That stooped erewhile our life's frail weed to wear !
Sun, clouds, and hills, all things Thou framest so fair,
With us are glad and gay, greeting the time.

The college of the lily leaves her sleep ;
The gray tower rocks and trembles into sound,
Dawn-smitten Memnon of a happier hour ;
Through faint-hued fields the silver waters creep ;
Day grows, birds pipe, and robed anew and crowned,
Green Spring trips forth to set the world aflower.

TO THE RIGHT REVEREND RICHARD DURNFORD, LORD BISHOP OF CHICHESTER, ON ST RICHARD'S DAY M.DCCCLXXXXII

Dicit quidem Petrus Ravennas, quod ipsa sæpe sanctorum nomina meritum indicant, testantur insignia ; Ricardus igitur etymologice potest dici, quasi Ridens, Carus *et* Dulcis . . . *ut metrice merito de ipso dicatur —*

> *Nominis in primo rides, dulcescis in imo,*
> *Si medium quæris, carus amicus eris.—*

Acta Sanctorum : Vita Sti Ricardi Cicestrensis.

RICHARD OF CHICHESTER

R ICHARD of Chichester, so ran the style
　　Of him who now six centuries away,
　Ruling Cicestria's 'realm' with gentle sway,
Sent light and peace out o'er our troubled isle,
His very name the record of his smile,
　　And of his sweetness and his charm, they say ;
　So ran the style, and so it runs to-day,
Though the saint sleeps beneath the hallowed pile ;

For still a Richard fills Cicestria's throne,
　　Whose ninetieth year mellows and not impairs
　　The ruler wise, learn'd scholar, faithful priest,
Courtly and kind and dear to all his own,
　　Friends who shall yet, if God so grant their prayers,
　　Send him more greetings on his namesake Feast.

(Regnum seems to have been the Roman name for Chichester.)

'WHERE TRUE JOYS ARE TO BE FOUND'

TIME was I yearned for happiness,
Time was I burned for fame,
Nor marked the Love and loveliness
Unsought, unbought that came :

Now happiness seems emptiness,
And fame a fickle breath,
And only Love and loveliness
Have promise over Death.

THE POINT OF SPRING

'TWAS that sweet moment of the year
   When first the seasons' hopes appear,
When through black boughs of winter seen
   Spring shimmers in a gauze of green.

His pushing heir not yet installed
   The guiltless cuckoo shyly called,
And like a fountain pulsing strong
   Larks towered and dropped on jets of song ;

Nodded beneath the sheltering hill
   In the low breeze the daffodil,
And pink the budding almond stood
   Blushing at her own hardihood ;

While on the down so harsh and bare
   But yesterday, see everywhere
Pale stars in purple morning set,
   The primrose with the violet !

E   25

HESPERIDES

ALL AMIDST THE GARDENS FAIR
OF HESPERUS AND HIS DAUGHTERS THREE
THAT SING ABOUT THE GOLDEN TREE

M ISTRESS Rachel, Mistress Ruth,
 Dancing down the ways of youth
By the dancing rills of truth,
Fairy music lead your measure,
Bring you to the hidden treasure
And the oracles of sooth,
Bid all sprites of evil vanish,
Gnome and Kobold ban and banish,
Charm each dragon head uncouth!

So they danced among their roses,
 Whom the Grecian tale discloses,
 In the golden-fruited garden
 Where the watchful snake was warden,
 Daughters of the sunset West,
 Magic maidens ever lilting,

26

Magic bowers never wilting,
While the sunset flashed and bickered
And the sparkling ocean flickered
And the silver Star of Even
Hung above the crimson heaven,
And the whirling world had rest.

Till there came the hero presence
Breaking on their charmèd pleasaunce
From the lands of work and pain,
Quelled the fierce unsleeping warden,
Plucked the fruitage of the garden
For a gift at Wisdom's fane ;
For a gift and for a token
That the lulling spell was broken,
All the careless years completed,
All their golden nonage fleeted,
And the star that lit to dreaming
Must for busy morn be beaming,
And the world must whirl again.

Dancing down the ways of youth
By the dancing rills of truth,
Fairy music lead your measure,

Bring you to the hidden treasure
And the oracles of sooth,
Bid all sprites of evil vanish,
Gnome and Kobold ban and banish,
Charm each dragon head uncouth ;
Mistress Rachel, Mistress Ruth !

Christmas, 1895.

A NEW YEAR'S GREETING

DEAR friends, who from your aëry home
    Watch all the glancing fates that fleet
In light and shade o'er tower and dome
       Of Oxford at your feet—

Green Spring that smiles through tears of rain,
    Or golden Summer's gorgeous glow—
Red Autumn on the fiery vane,
       White Winter still with snow :—

Thames vale in morning vapour drest,
    Noon brooding o'er the sultry High,
The Poet's Tree by Cumnor crest
       Etched on the evening sky :—

You scan our scene, you hear our noise—
    A sound of many changing chimes,
Now sad with grief, now glad with joys,
       The echo of our times :

29

You see us through a happy haze
    Of new delight, of old content,
But are you mindful of the days
        That here below you spent ?

Do you to-night perchance remember
    A fragrant hour, a summer moon,—
Will you watch with us in December,
        As once you watched in June ?

Midsummer-midnight 'twas—no word
    Spoke from the sleeping moon-blanched tower,
Only the soul the secret heard
        Of that fate-laden hour.

Midwinter-midnight 'tis, and, hark !
    From merry spire and turret ring
A hundred chimes through all the dark—
        What burthen do they sing ?

' A year is flying, sighing, flowing, going,
    A dear old year, a kind old year :—
A year is meeting, greeting, showing, growing,
    A bright, a light New Year.

'New homes, new hopes, new joy, and if new trouble,
  Love old and new, in joy, in trouble too :
Happy the single life, happier the double,
    Happy the old, happier the new :
    Two loves for one, four friends for two.'

L'ENVOI

Then hail, dear friends, thrice o'er, and let this letter
  Writ in the old year bid welcome to the new :
Good was the old, but may the new be better,
    Dear friends, for us and you !

Magdalen College :
New Year's Eve, 1890.

TO THE BRIDE

WITH A COPY OF ROBERT BRIDGES'
'SHORTER POEMS'

TO the bride
   Her friends two
   Old and new
Wedlock-tied

Send this tome,
   With all message
   Fair, to presage
Her new home.

Of Oxford's best
   He who wrote
   Each sweet note,—
He who pressed,—

He who bound ;—
   May she find
   It to her mind,
As they've found !

TO J. C. S.

ENVOY TO A BIRTHDAY ODE

DEAR Lady, take this little song,
    Not over-wise though all too long ;
  As tiny straws flung up in air
  May show what way strong winds do fare,
  So little words ill-chosen and weak
  The heart's deep voice may faintly speak.

Time was I found thy stately mien
  As of a gracious distant queen ;
  Now drawing nearer to thy throne,
  With growing years emboldened grown,
  I fain take courage to record
  The debt that all these years afford ;
  And though no words on any day
  Nor any deeds can all repay,
  Bid boyhood's chivalry find end
  In the true service of a friend.

Davos Platz,
    26th August, 1884.

TO J. C. S.

A BIRTHDAY ODE

WHILOME I wrote a little song,
    Not wise, I said, though all too long,
  A little song great debt to pay,
  How great nor short nor long could say.

  A stately gracious queen you seemed
  When youth confirmed what boyhood dreamed ;
  Now youth to ampler manhood changed
  O'er wider fields of life has ranged ;
  Some flowers he finds grown fruit, some yet
  Flowering, and still the ancient debt
  Exceeds the utmost of his store,
  And you are worthier than before ;
  So little words ill-chosen and weak
  The heart's deep voice once more must speak.

Ah ! can it be a lustre's flown
  Since then we gathered at your throne ?
  How full the years, how fleet the tides,
  How much is gone, how much abides,

What loss in gain, what gain in loss,
What siftings of the gold from dross,
What planting and what watering hours,
What increase from the holier powers,
What hopes grown memories, what fears,
What tender joys, what tenderer tears
Too sacred for a holiday,
Yet never from our hearts away,
While that sweet heaven-uplifted star
Smiles on her earthly home from far !

So take, dear Lady of this day,
Once more the tribute of a lay
And gratitude how poorly drest,
With five years' added interest,
Nay, doubled now by that sweet tone
The over-echo or my own ;
For listen, and you'll hear it come
A response o'er the seas of home
In sweet accord to all I say
From her that should be here to-day ;
When all and each who call you friend
Or dearer names, your court attend
In act or heart, with blithest mien

35

And festal garb to greet their queen,
Whose crown is wisdom as of old
And courtesy her orb of gold,
Whose sceptre bright Ithuriel's lance,
Truth kindling truth where'er it glance.

Long may you reign, and long may we
Or young or old your lieges be !
And for your humble loyal bard,
If neither fate nor you be hard,
Thus much he hopes, thus much he prays,
Your royal laurel for his lays,
And that on some far birthday he
May see and share your Jubilee !

Davos Platz,
26th August, 1889.

LINES FOR A SUNDIAL

Meditatur Homo.

DAWNE TO DARKE
GRADE BY GRADE
SHADOWES MARKE.

*

Monet Solarium.

SHADOWE HARKE
WHAT YS SAYDE !

*

Monitio.

THYNGES DIVRNALLE
BIN A SHADE
OF ETERNALLE.

37

ANTHEM

WRITTEN FOR AND SUNG AT THE MEMORIAL SERVICE AT
FROGMORE, 14TH DECEMBER 1896

> *Yea, like as a father pitieth his own children,*
> *even so is the Lord merciful unto them that fear*
> *Him. For He knoweth whereof we are made,*
> *He remembereth that we are but dust.*

WORKS of earth and words of air,
    Dust to dust, and breath to breath,
All we are, and all we were,
    He who made remembereth.

Nought abideth, this world's scheme
    Perisheth and vanisheth,
Passing like a broken dream
    Waking none remembereth.

Grief abideth, years returning
    To the hearts He chasteneth
Bring again the tears of mourning ;
    He who wept remembereth.

Faith abideth, even on earth
    Faithfully who laboureth,
Lo, his life hath endless worth,
    And his Lord remembereth.

Hope abideth, like a star,
    When the darkness deepeneth,
Guiding to that country far
    Pilgrim zeal remembereth.

Love abideth, Love in heaven,
    Love on earth, can conquer death,
So His love, by whom is given
    All our love, remembereth.

Lord, remember, Lord, forget not !
    Howsoe'er forgetful we,
Lord, remember, Jesu, let not
    Our frail nature fall from Thee !

39

NATURAL RELIGION

I WANDERED by the shining river's side,
 Tenderly after Spring's first warming rain
 Blue the heaven, and blue the mirroring tide ;
 From end to end of his restored domain
 The steely swallow swooped ; tufted and pied
 With blossom white and gold the meadow plain,
 And fringed with rush and reed, whereby did glide
 Sweet Thames aripple with rustling glistening train.

I wandered by the steaming river's side,
 Sultry and sick the air, a stagnant thread
 The shrunken stream erewhile so flush and wide
 From pool to pool crawled in his shrivelled bed ;
 Vanished the springing flowers, yellow and dried
 A stubble of withered grass showed in their stead,
 And scarce Thames' honest face could be descried
 With scummy froth and rotting weed o'erspread.

I wandered by the river's side once more ;
 As to some mask of death face-cloth and pall

The chill white mists clung close, an iron floor
Hard, cold as death itself, with icy wall
Pent the invisible stream from shore to shore ;
Silence was over all, death everywhere,
Death desolate, mute, motionless and frore,
On sullen earth, clogged flood and starving air.

Again I wandered by the river's shore ;
Motion was there again, tumult and throes,
For all the surface heaved and cracked and tore
Riven and splintered into jagged floes
That gnashed and justled as they downward bore,
Griding and scoring all the tender bank
And sweeping flotage or wreck and drift before
The ruining hurry of their turbulent rank.—

Then came a warm wet wind, incessantly
The rain descended and the tempest beat
On sodden grass and black unsheltering tree,
Or changed to colder airs with hail and sleet
Lashing the wrinkled flood and shivering lea,
Till all the cleansing cycle was complete,
And joy returned and bright tranquillity,
And to the stream once more I bent-my feet :

Nor less than this, nor less than death, I cried,
    Than death and dissolution must befall,
    Ere earth could see again his summer pride,
    Or spring her budding maidenhood recall ;
    Fair things must fade that beauty may abide,
    Love is the purpose as the source of strife,
    —So closely link the powers that look so wide,—
And life death's death, and death the life of life !

TO L. R.

WITH A COPY OF ROBERT BRIDGES' 'SHORTER POEMS'

TAKE, friend of all that's good and fair,
   This book of daintiest verse,
And let each coy retirèd air
   Its music rare rehearse.

The silver Thames by summer kis't,
   The rustling brakes of Spring
Or Autumn woods when gales are whist,
   Such songs as these they sing.

Such songs in England's flowering day
   Made merry England brave,
From honied Chaucer shrewdly gay
   To Wither blithely grave.

43

FOR ———

LEAVING GRAYTHWAITE BY WINDERMERE

DEAR the gray walls hid in the greenwood side
    Cresting the sunny shore,
That sleeping sees the snowy canvas glide
    And hears the oar ;

Dear the swift stream that tumbling through the glen
    Scurries across the mead,
Fit emblem of the restless life of men
    With peace to end its speed ;

Dear the high moor with purple heath o'erblown,
    With bracken and with ling,
Haunts only to the screaming plover known
    Or the wild hawk's wide wing ;

There lonely straying ofttimes have I vowed
    My friendship to the rill,
Or sworn me sister to the wandering cloud
    Or far-off solemn hill.

44

Ah sheltering garden of my girlhood's day,
    Ah vocal solitude,
Into the world of men I take my way
    With all its murmurs rude ;

Your charmèd woods I leave, yet ere I go
    Into the hum and strife
May something of your tranquil beauty flow
    And pass into my life !

So when I weary with the stifling breath
    And deafen with the noise,
Shall come to save me from the spirit's death
    The memory of your joys ;

Tired of the town my fancy's feet shall tread
    Once more the upland sod,
And lead once more the days my childhood led
    With Nature and with God.

AN EXCUSE

YOU asked me, friend, to send a Sonnet,
    I wrote that I would think upon it,
But Love is neither sold nor bought,
And sonnets do not come with thought,
Unless the touch of fire be given
The Muse alone can filch from Heaven ;
So though my answer linger late,
I crave your patience still to wait
Till sunnier hours and skies more kind
Befriend a something torpid mind.
When this relentless winter yields,
And cowslips tuft your Pencombe fields,
And when in Maudlin May is born
With chant and chime and dissonant horn,
And trees grow green and rivers glisten,
And for the cuckoo's call we listen,
And larger light gives larger scope
To soul and sense, why then we'll hope
The month and Muse may me inspire
With happier chance to prove the lyre,
And then may be I'll send a Sonnet,
For in meantime I'll think upon it.

TO HENRY OLIVE DANIEL OF WORCESTER COLLEGE,
WITH A COPY OF THE WORKS OF SAMUEL DANIEL
THE POET

DANIEL, well-lettered son of Somerset,
    And even as he who did these lays indite
    'Well-languaged,' take them, yours they are by right
Of name and nurture, and hereafter let—
Lest we fair Delia's Petrarch should forget—
    Some choice exemplar stand for our delight,
    Type, paper, margin, all things, trimly dight,
Your *Excudebat* for their warrant set !

For you enrich the poet-shrining shelf
    With daintiest treasures old and new, and give
    In many a nice and justly-ordered page
Back to mechanic days of haste and pelf
    The tasteful Tudor touch,—so these shall live
    Green as their shire and yours from age to age.

TO AMERICA

WRITTEN DURING THE SICKNESS OF PRESIDENT GARFIELD,
SEPTEMBER 1881

DEAR second home beyond the misty sea,
    Shore where the brethren of our fathers sought
    With that chaste bride for whom our fathers fought
From storms and foes escaped in peace to be :
That bride whom all too soon fate's irony
    Bade their sons choose both peace and kin before,
    Then when not England on her children war,
But England's blinded rulers did decree.

Dear home and folk, whom still one tongue assures
    Blood of our blood, who know spite waves and years
    One fealty to one freedom ours and yours,
Now in your night of trials and of fears
    While light is not and sorrow's ache endures,
Our prayers you have—may you not need our tears !

ST. PETER'S HOME

TO suffer or to succour, 'tis the school
　　Where best we learn what things have truest worth ;
　　Not man's frail glories nor his frailer mirth,
Nor all that doth his purblind sense befool ;
But to discern by Heaven's inmost rule
　　Flowers in the desert, manna amid dearth,
　　In tears the baptism of the soul's new birth,
In pain the angel of the healing pool.

Therefore this House is even God's Hostelry,
　　Where with yet throbbing limbs His pilgrims wait,
　　　　Under the wall of His own City of Peace,
Till thou, the great Apostle of the key,
　　Shall at His bidding ope the golden gate,
　　　　And all their labour and their longing cease.

WILLIAM COLLINS

SCHOLAR OF WINCHESTER 1733-40
COMMONER OF QUEEN'S 1740-41.   DEMY OF MAGDALEN 1741-44

NIGHTINGALE poet, all too delicate
   For the world's noon ; shy student, with the fair
   Vision of ancient Hellas and the rare
Magic of her lost lyres impassionate ;
Thou for a while of freedom, love, and fate,
   Nature, and man's regret, didst trill thine air,
   Thy bosom to the thorn, but could'st not bear
Of raptured frenzy the o'erteeming freight :

Yet for thy suffering large reward was given,
   In weakness to forerun corrival strength
      And catch the music of the coming days,
From thy mad cell to hear the voice of Heaven
   After earth's Babel, and on earth at length
      Pure laurels and thy brethren's nicest praise.

50

EARLY TRAVEL

SWEPT by the breaths of memory
    From those far heights that roll,
What thousand shimmering pictures lie
    Glassed in thy depths, O soul!

What cherished scenes from that blithe day
    When first by happy chance,
Our careless trio took its way
    Beyond the seas to France :

When whirled across a weary land
    All day on wheels of fire,
At even how glad we saw them stand,
    The peaks of our desire.

What towering barriers' shadowy sleep
    Lulled by the pastoral tune
Of tinkling kine that trampled deep
    In the lush fields of June!

What clustering huts that barred the way,
　　What modest faces shy,
What simple souls' untrammelled play,
　　True seed of Arcady !

What scented pine-trees' whispered moan,
　　What chime of silver rills
'Mid flowerets pure as blow alone
　　Upon the sacred hills !

To rise, to climb, beneath the night,
　　And while the day was born,
How flushed and paled till all was bright
　　Horn after icy horn !

How watched a silent goddess grand
　　The mountain of the Rose ;
How Cervin ramped twixt land and land,
　　An obelisk of snows!

To pause beneath the sombre arch
　　Cool in its noontide gloom,
And seem to catch the echoing march
　　Of the stern sons of Rome ;

Or make beneath Italian sky
    The dusty defile ring,
Racing the flood that thundered by
    Swoln with the spates of spring;

Lo, piled upon the mountain side
    The towers that Virgil drew,
" Rivers 'neath ancient bulwarks glide,"—
    That master-hand how true!

And ah, what gentler dear delights
    By thy loved lake Lucerne,
Slow sailing under dreaming heights
    To watch thy waters burn,

When evening on thy pathways glowed,
    And streamed by spire and bridge,
And distant dim Pilatus showed
    More soft his traitor's ridge!

YOUTH'S ECLIPSE

SICK Autumn spreads his magic tints
       O'er earth and sea,
The landscape's hectic splendour hints
       The close to be;
One hue the smouldering forest paints
       And scarlet skies,
In mist the narrowing evening faints
       And fades and flies,
Cold vapours rise a thousand shadows blending
       Of gold and gray,
And sad and swift in dim mysterious ending
       Burns down the day.
My soul, my soul, why also dies thy laughter
       In chills and fears?
Why dost thou strain and yearn to follow after
       With sighs and tears?
Further than night and winter thou must follow
       The goal to see,

54

Else Spring returned all vain and Summer hollow
    To thee will be:
Once hast thou wept o'er Autumn and o'er even,
    Thou'rt past the door
Of Eden : farewell happy early Heaven,
    For evermore!

BRISTOL AND CLIFTON

O SWEET to hear and feel their strife
  That battle in the human cause,
  And make their mother Nature's laws,
Work out their higher, richer life.

Ay, sweet the whirring of the loom,
  And tramping hoof and rolling wain,
  And feet that pass and come again,
And dusky, overhanging gloom.

And sweet to see beside the quays
  The stately ships from distant climes,
  And hear the pealing steeple-chimes
Half drowned in din of thronging ways.

O sweet to leave the common pen,
  To feel a world of wider span,
  To cast the appanage of man,
And think of other things than men.

Ay, sweet the sultry summer sleep,
　　With chirring birds in brake and fern,
　　With silver laughter of the burn,
With distant plashing of the deep.

Or sweet from off some breezy wold
　　That crowns the rugged-pillared scar,
　　To catch beyond the woods afar
The sunset ocean shot with gold.

THE MICROCOSM

DARK against the sky
    Rises the mountain wall,
    But bright, how bright
    In the summer light
    Dashed into white with fall on fall
    The streamlet hurries by !

And here will I lay me down,
    Little stream, for a while by thee,
    Thou one among many, unnoticed, unknown,
    Of all save yon wandering bee,
    Or these flies whose world is this pool of thine,
    Wherein to live and to love, to rejoice and repine.

Yes ! here will I lay me down
    By this pool and this fall of thine,
    And watch the droplets gather and glitter and slip
    From the pendent mosses that fringe the edge
    Of thy tiny channel, or tip
    Some infinitesimal ledge.

Since not Niagara's self
>Is more wondrous one whit than this,
>Though it swoop a sea from a continent shelf
>To plunge in an ocean abyss :

>For these delicate spikes of flowers,
>And tremulous bents of grass,
>Are waved by the self-same breeze
>That sways the giant trees,
>Or sweeps the Alpine pass,
>Or buffets the soaring pride of sky-built city towers :
>And each fairy filament,
>And feathery frond of fern,
>Is strung of no other element
>Than builds yon mountain chain,
>Or moons that wax and wane,
>Or suns and stars that burn :

And were this to stay in its course,
>Or these waters turn back their way,
>The sun would stop and the moon would stay,
>And the stars that are whirled by the self-same force
>Through the cycles of months and of years, of night
>>and of day.

Ay, wondrous indeed art thou,
 But how more wonderful I,
 For thou wilt flow as thou flowest now,
 And wear the hills till they sink and are low,
 And through changes endure for ever and on,
 For thy force and thy stuff will never be gone,
 But I shall shortly die !

THE EVERLASTING NO

THOU who hast seen for once and all the vision,
    Thou who hast felt high discontent
And known the bitter sweet of great ambition,
    Not for these short-lived follies thou wast meant.

Yet which to follow of the striving voices,
    Faith, knowledge, nature, still to meet
Surfeit in pleasure, in faith superstition,
    In knowledge weariness, in love deceit?

Forth to the wilderness? Ah I see only
    Desert winds shaking the desert reeds:
Ignorant and thirsting still and lonely
    Shall solitude suffice my thousand needs?

What though the inner eye be filled with seeing,
      What though the mountain and the plain be great,
Only to think and brood in dreams of being,
      This cannot solve the riddle of our fate.

Sight of the stars and conscious sense of duty,
      These are but drops in the still vacant heart,
These have I known and felt and loved their beauty
      With half my soul, nor filled the other part.

THE GOLDEN AGE

A Y ME ! ay me ! how sweet
With eyes of yearning far behind us cast,
Tired eyes atingle with the bitter blast,
Tired eyes and sore with all the glare and heat
That doth so fiercely beat
On our poor brows who wage
Here in the blinding dust and sharp turmoil
Hard warfare, wearying strife,
And live our workday life
Of unremitting toil
In this our iron age,
How sweet, how glad to turn us to the past,
How glad, how sweet to gaze
With yearning eyes far backward cast,
On those fair seasons of the world's first dawn,
And scenes so far withdrawn,

As through a golden haze
Lit with a rich yet tempered light,
Till our outwearied sight
Be comforted feasting on the green of grass,
And violet gray of sky,
And waters hyaline,
And vistas softly lucent wherein pass
Fair forms of men and women by,
And shadowy ampler shapes than these, divine !

FOR A CHILDREN'S GAME

For a Little Girl

I AM a modest Violet—
 Dew tears of joy my dark eyes wet,
 My fragrance fills my lowly nest,
 The humblest oft are happiest.

For a Girl

I AM a stately Foxglove tall—
 I ring my nodding bells and call—
 Ho busy bees that wandering roam,
 Here's honey, honey, for your home !

For a Boy

A BULLRUSH I on river bank—
 Stand with my men in serried rank,
 And straight and proud keep watch and ward
 O'er all who pass the shining ford.

GREEK CHILDREN'S SWALLOW SONG

Ἦλθ᾽, ἦλθε χελιδών

THE swallow is here, is here
    Bringing the joyous spring,
Bringing the joyous year
On bosom white and sable wing.

Quick, out with the kneaded cake
    From the house of plenteous ease,
And a cup of wine our thirst to slake
And a basket filled with cheese !
Nor on white bread nor brown
Does the swallow look down.

Shall we take or shall we be gone ?
    If thou givest aught—
    But woe if not,
We will not let thee alone.

Shall we take the door or the lintel
Or thy wife who sits within ?
We'll easily carry her off,
She is so small and thin ;
But if thou givest a portion,
Great may thy portion be.

Ope, ope to the swallow the door !
We are no sages with foreheads hoar
But only children are we.

Athenæus, viii. 360 c.

τῶν ἐν Θερμοπύλαις θανόντων

R ENOWNED their lot and fair their fame,
    Thermopylæ's great dead ;
    Their grave a shrine is, theirs for pity acclaim,
    And memory in the stead
    Of tears ; a shroud
    So rich, so proud,
    Nor mouldering stain
    Nor conquering time shall blot ;
    The ' Heroes' Close ' this plot
    All Hellas' glory to its tenant hath ta'en.

So witnesses Leonidas, the King
    Of Sparta, he who left behind
    Rich ornament of valorous mind
    And praise that bards shall never cease to sing.

Simonides ap. Diod. Sic. xi. 11.

'MY LATE ESPOUSED SAINT'

BELOVED she moved among us,
　　Belovèd she lies in her grave,
To a home, to a husband's bosom
　　Came never a bride more brave.

Tomb of a buried mortal
　　Count not her barrow then,
As the shrines of the gods are honoured
　　Be it honoured of men !

Climbing the crookèd way
　　There shall the traveller say,
'She died on a day for her husband
　　And now she's a spirit in heaven ;
　　All hail, Lady, thy blessing
　　Here to us be it given !'

　　　　Euripides: Alcestis; vv. 991—1004.

69

VANITY FAIR

HIM, Parmeno, I reckon happiest
    Who, looking calmly on this glorious pageant
Of common sun, stars, water, cloud, and fire
Awhile, soon takes his journey whence he came.
For these, if thou should live to be an hundred,
Thou'lt still see there, or if thy years be few ;
And aught more glorious thou'lt never see.

Count then our time on earth as a World's Fair,
Where mankind gather from their several homes,
—A chaffering crowd, thieves, dice, the fun o' the fair,—
The first to pack his traps and leave his inn
Takes the best victual and the good word of all ;
But he who lingers late, cleaned out and broken,
Finds sour old age and want come surely on him
Bandied about 'mid enemies and snares :
Who comes to stay, goes sorrily to's grave.

From Menander's 'Changeling.'

A GREEK ADDISON

Cf. ' Spectator,' No. 26

WHENEVER thou would'st know thy real worth,
Mark, as thou goest, the gravestones of the dead!
There shrunk to ashes and a puff of dust,
Lie kings and kesars once the great and wise,
And they whom wealth and they whom birth made
 boastful,
Or their great glory or their shining beauty,
But nought of all could fence them against time,
Mortal they were and found one common grave ;
Look on the dead and know man's true estate!

From an unknown play of Menander.

THE OLD YACHT

THAT craft, my friends, you there behold,
  The fastest thing afloat of old,
If you'll believe her tale, was she ;
'No timber ever swam the sea
But she could give it the go-by,
Were need with oar or sail to fly ' ;
A truth fell Adria's beach allows,
Aye, and the Circlet Isles, she vows,
And glorious Rhodes and savage Thrace,
Propontis, and thy wreckful race,
Pontus, where she a ship to-day
Was once a waving wood, she'll say,
Whose vocal tresses whispered oft
Upon Cytorus' ridge aloft.

Pontic Amastris and ye rocks
Cytorian hight that bear the box,
Ye knew, ye know, and ye can tell
How since the hour her birth befell,

Yours was the top on which she stood,
—So much she claims,—and yours the flood
First wet her maiden oars, anon
Through chafing channels many a one
She bore her lord, howe'er the gale
On port or starboard woo'd the sail,
Or if heaven's influence following fair
Strained either sheet with equal air ;
Nor ever vow to gods of shore
For her did crew or captain pour,
While from old Ocean's farthest bound
To this clear lake her way she found.
But that is ancient history,
To-day in harbour she's laid by
To rest and rust self-dedicate
To Castor and to Castor's mate.

Catullus : Carm. iv.

THE POET TO THE ORATOR

TULLY, of all Rome's progeny
   Most eloquent that e'er can be,
Or is, or was in history,
Full thanks to you Catullus gives
The very poorest bard that lives,
Of all Rome's bards as much the worst
As you of all her bar the first.

Catullus: Carm. xlix.

PEREUNT ET IMPUTANTUR

DEAR Martial, if with you I could
    Taste days of gladness free from care,
Arrange my moments as I would,
Leisure, and life worth living, share,
On halls and houses of the great,
Dull glories of heraldic state,
Crabbed cases in the dismal court,
On these, on these we would not wait :
But walk and talk and book and sport,
The cool alcove, the shady tree,
The bath, the Maiden Fount, should be
Business and haunt for you and me.

To-day, alas ! nor you nor I
Can be ourselves ; the bright hours meant
To be so good, they pass and fly,
Still scored against us ' had and spent.'

Ah, is not this the moral, say,
He who *might* live must not delay ?

Martial: Epig. v. 20.

75

EPITAPH

BENEATH this rising mound entombed is laid
    Æolis' Canace ; poor little maid,
Her seventh winter was her very last ;
O sin, O shame ! yet stay, you weep too fast ;
Life's transient term here is no place to blame,
Sad was her death, more sad the way it came :
A wasting plague her beauty reft away
And made her darling face its helpless prey,
Ruthless, her very kisses to consume,
Nor give her lips unrifled to the tomb :
So sudden must he swoop, the vulture god,
At least he might some other way have trod ;
Nay, Death made haste her sweet voice to imprison,
Lest that dear tongue should coax e'en the grim grave
    to listen.

Martial: Epig., xi. 81.

'WER NIE SEIN BROD'

(*From Goethe*)

WHO never ate with tears his bread,
    Who never in drear midnight hours
Hath sat him weeping on his bed,
    He knows you not, ye Heavenly Powers.

You bring poor mortals to the birth,
    You let them sin, and then to sorrow
You hand them o'er, for on your earth
    All they must surely pay who borrow !

THE DISDAINFUL SHEPHERDESS

(*From Goethe*)

'TWAS a cloudless April morrow,
    And the Shepherdess went singing,
Young and fair and without sorrow,
    Setting all the meadows ringing,
So la la! lay ralla . . .

Thyrsis offered for a kissie
    Of his lambs a pair or more—
Paused and glanced the artful missie,
    Laughed and lilted as before,
So la la! lay ralla . . .

Then a second ribbons offered,
    And a third his heart would tender:
Heart or ribbons, all they proffered,
    She did still one answer render,—
'Twas—*la la! lay ralla . . .*

ES FÄLLT EIN STERN HERUNTER

(*From Heine*)

FALLETH a shooting star
    From his sparkling heights above,
I see it from afar,
    It is the star of love !

Fall from the apple trees
    Both leaf and blossom thick,
Cometh the mocking breeze,
    Tosseth with wanton trick.

Singeth a swan i' the mere
    And roweth to and fro,
With song that dies on the ear
    Sinketh the flood below.

All is so still and dark,
    Both leaf and bloom are flown,
Burnt out the smouldering spark,
    The swan hath ended her moan.

www.ingramcontent.com/pod-product-compliance
Lightning Source LLC
Chambersburg PA
CBHW020048030726
47499CB00007B/2642